Summer in Sannomacl

Paws outstretched and
and focuses it onto the
three hundred years, n
roof is warm and that's

The sound of merchants calling from their open shop
frontages, with deep bows and broad smiles, fills his pointed
ears.

'Irasshaimase!'

Slowly losing interest in the human activity, he curls up
into a ball and lets the distant sound of cicadas—their low
chattering to one another—help him to close his eyes
instead. As he does, he catches sight of one of the
merchants splashing water onto the street, almost soaking
the feet of two kimono-clad women who handle the issue as
though graceful swans continuing to flow downstream.
Soon the cat will jump down from his rooftop, quench his
thirst and cool down—his ginger fur being the perfect
conduit for the summer heat.

For now, though, he shall return to slumber; the bustling
street will happily go on without his participation. The days
will meander by in the same leisurely style, until autumn
beckons and his rooftop becomes carpeted with amber
leaves. Then shall come the blanket of snow and retreating
indoors, until a sprinkling of cherry blossom reunites him
with his favourite place on earth—the roof of the saké shop
on the Sannomachi, Takayama, Japan. The cycle of the
seasons repeating every year, the cycle of his day destined to
be just the same tomorrow.

Rocky Bay by Andrew Anderson

Grjótafjörður, or 'Rocky Bay'—it's not on many of the Icelandic maps, and it's not on the ones in your tourist's guide.

With only four shops—which operate with unpredictable opening hours—the harbour will become a frequent destination for you, at least on the rare occasions when it isn't raining. You could try to enjoy the view of the mountains beyond the slate-grey sea but standing downwind from the fish factory means you won't stay long.

Or you could wander past the church but, apparently abandoned, it'll never be open regardless of the timing of your visits. There is beauty to be found here though, if you look for it: the sunshine, when it eventually breaks through the rain clouds to illuminate the toy-like colours on the metal houses; the puffins, protecting their precious catch from piratical skuas; the group of old women on their twice-weekly pilgrimage to the fisherman's memorial, to lay flowers in memory of their drowned husbands, sons and brothers.

I recommend that you find Gummi's café. I could tell you the street name, but it's easier to follow the sweet and warming aromas of sugar, cinnamon and cardamom wafting from the kitchen window, as freshly rolled *kleinur* is being deep-fried.

You'll find me sitting at the aged table in the corner, sipping from a cup filled with the blackest, strongest and most glorious coffee I have ever tasted. Sit down beside me.

Mark this place on your map, and then upon your heart.

Tolworth Treasure by Alison Fure

Tolworth Court Farm was an inspiration to the nature writer Richard Jefferies, and last year we followed in his footsteps, navigating pathways through the farm's fields.

The last time Jefferies left his home to walk this route, he reminded us of 2,000 lapwings and the abundance of skylarks regularly encountered and recorded in his weekly columns for the *Pall Mall Gazette* (later published as *Nature Near London*). The lapwing may be gone, but the underlying fertile, wetness of the ground is evidenced by stands of three reed species, now growing in fields alongside the river.

Here existed his favourite 'thinking places' such as an aspen by the Hogsmill Brook that became a site of almost daily pilgrimage. He saw nature not only as a medicine for his ailing body but as a 'balm for the restless, unquiet mind'. We no longer encounter the trout in the Hogsmill—whose side he once took over the angler's—but it does very well for chub and barbel.

He would approve of the cattle that we hope will graze the farm in future. He was tormented by the livestock beaten by drovers along the Ewell Road with their 'great heads swaying side to side'. After the railway opened in 1840, there was little reason to continue maintaining the toll-free drove roads—with their double hedgerows—and many were lost, the livestock forced into worse conditions on the trucks. Last year, whilst we picnicked and read poems in the drove, we pledged to keep the Farm intact.

All quotations are from Nature Near London *by Richard Jefferies (original edition 1893).*

Hidden Gem by Mel Davies

Come closer and let me take you into my secret place.

A survivor of the bombings of war and subsequent bad planning decisions that mirror its inhabitants.

Tucked within this maze of hotchpotch architecture and Victorian workmen's dwellings you can easily miss the iron gate, but it opens onto a wiggly path of misplaced stones with an abundance of flowering pots lining the way.

On entering you discover the smallest one bedroom terraced cottages, all with front gardens leading onto this central path. Each house unique, with its own character and personality propping up the next. A crowded mouth with too many teeth.

Now follow the path towards the end. A community garden, complete with bench, table and barbecue await, enticing you to relax.

Stop now and listen.

Soak in the stillness.

Is that a thrush or blackbird song?

A rustling of leaves as a cat prowls through the undergrowth, watchful and alert.

Here in the heart of a city neighbourhood lies an urban tranquility.

The seasons come with cherry blossom and trailing nasturtiums.

Magnolia flowers and apple trees bearing fruits rejoice in the rich soil from the exploration and nurseries of the past. The autumnal crackling of leaves under foot turning into the barren winter months. A canopy sheltering the early buds of crocus and snowdrops.

So welcome dear reader to Choumert Square.

Urban paradise, hidden gem, a lost neighbourhood that still survives in the heart of Peckham SE15.

The Spell is Broken by Paul Chown

A woman disappeared and then another appeared—naked—in Richmond Park, London yesterday.

Lisa Pryce, 59, was in the Pembroke Lodge Café, where she'd been taken for first aid after apparently being bitten by a rabbit. Husband Greg, 58, left her with daughter Martha, 26, while he fetched the car to take her to hospital.

Lisa's family say she noticed the rabbit following them. Despite their warnings, she reached down to stroke it. The rabbit then bit her hand before running off.

As Martha waited, her mother became agitated and delirious. After fifteen minutes Lisa ran out of the café before Martha could stop her, disappearing into the trees.

Meanwhile, walkers found a naked woman near the park's Ham Gate exit. This woman—who identified herself as Alice Kemp—was fiftyish, dishevelled and confused.

'She kept saying: "The spell is broken,"' says Jon Cohen, who gave Alice his jacket and phoned for help.

An hour later police and an ambulance arrived for Lisa. Police combed the park, finding her clothes under a clump of trees. Her jacket and jeans were zipped, with her top and underwear inside them. Her socks were inside her shoes.

There have been no sightings of Lisa, either by the public or on the gates' CCTV cameras. There is also no footage of Alice entering the park, and police have been unable to find her clothes. They have appealed to the public for any information.

Tunnel to another time by Amanda Tuke

Both restless and looking for somewhere to be still, I'm drawn to an old favourite. Through the gate into the woods, I turn south along the old track bed towards the tunnel. The mouth is muzzled with metal gates, once an incongruous grey, then lovingly painted with bats whose furry faces are now beginning to lose out to rainbows slashed with zombie grins.

In the tree-walled cutting, the bench is submerged under sodden hornbeam fruits. So instead I stand there in shadow, soft breathing until my inner chatter ebbs.

A murmur of autumn wind whips up to a roar in the beech and ash boughs overhead. With a final decisive gust, fat gobbets of water are hurled down.

Up through the ash canopy, there's a glimpse of blue and late afternoon sunlight. Gilded wood pigeons deftly thread their way through the branches and a magpie chunters at me angrily from a hazel sapling.

From the tunnel, the faint echo of a steam train emerges, bringing a weary cargo of families back to London. They are all in their Sunday clothes, after a one shilling day out at the Crystal Palace. Children press faces against the carriage windows, eyes still wide perhaps from tight-rope walking feats, treasures from Egypt or the prehistoric monsters in the park.

An outburst of parakeets sees off my ghost train. Two walkers approach along the track, and I become self-conscious about my immobility. We pass, exchange a smile and then another gust and soaking drives me back to the gate.

Perpetuity by Carrie Dunne

Nestling on the side of a valley in France stands a traditional Breton cottage. Surrounded by fields of corn and grass, the cottage has witnessed the relentless coming and going of the seasons; seasons which formed and guided the secure, comfortable and predictable backdrop to our lives.

The spring months of bright sunrises and birdsong; of shared love in planting red geraniums and bicycling the twisty lanes with laughter and warm smiles.

The summer months of doors and windows thrown open; of outdoor feasting and long warm evenings lying close together under clear skies spotting shooting stars.

The autumn months of harvesting fruit for jam and root vegetables for warming soups; of collecting and organizing the woodpile ready for the colder months ahead.

The winter months of orange flame and crackles from the wood-burning stove; of cozy evenings snuggled under patchwork quilts touching hands across our twin armchairs.

Then one year, just as winter was turning to spring, death cast its dark shadow and our once secure, comfortable and predictable lives unraveled in grief.

Nestling on the side of a valley in France still stands a traditional Breton cottage. Surrounded by fields of corn and grass, the cottage continues to witness the relentless coming and going of the seasons; seasons which, for me, have now become tangled and meaningless.

And, just like me, the patchwork quilts and twin armchairs stand forlorn and discarded, clinging onto nothing more than precious memories.

Capel Cwmorthin: What remains in high places
by Ruth Bradshaw

Slate is everywhere here—in the steep track underfoot, the jagged piles towering overhead and the tumbled walls of ruined houses. Up ahead I can see the familiar jagged silhouette of the roofless chapel, with its distinctive long narrow glassless windows.

Most of the chapel's back wall has collapsed since my last visit and with the wind howling and the rain lashing down, it is easy to picture this happening. Inside, the floor is a jumble of stones with a few pieces of rotten wood sticking out. Reeds and grass grow in the few areas not covered by fallen rocks and the grey walls are speckled with mosses and ferns. Nature is gradually reclaiming the materials from which the building was made.

I stand for a few moments in a corner of the chapel with my eyes closed and imagine it as it would have been every Sunday for so many decades. The rows of wooden pews filled with worshippers, the smell of well-worn woollen clothing that never quite gets a chance to dry properly, the voices raised in harmony, singing in a language I do not understand and interspersed with the coughing and wheezing of lungs damaged by slate dust and the cold, damp living conditions.

What would those worshippers make of me and all the others who now walk and run through the mountains where once they lived and too many of them died? Did the beauty of their surroundings provide much compensation for such a harsh life?

All Change by Pennie Hedge

Slip away from the busy South Circular up a tarmacked path between wooden fences. Follow it past the T&RA hall and flimsy 70s flats. Above the concrete steps, the path steepens and then doglegs onto a hoggin track between railings; the air instantly cooler as the greenery leans in. See where ivy has climbed inside the hollow tubes to flower at their tips; listen for the wind singing in the pipes or rain ringing the tubular bells. At the top go through the wide kissing gate, broken back on its hinges, and down the steps, nosing the wood ahead. Breathe.

The eye jumps at the sight of a broad footbridge with its three massive timber frames. Halfway across, a much graffitied notice shows a picture Pissarro painted at that very spot: a steam train chuffing up the cutting from Lordship Lane station. Now ash and hornbeam fill that view; station and iron rails long gone.

At the far end of the bridge stand two soaring oaks, planted by man or jay a hundred or more years ago. They flourished, spread their canopies when the railway cutting was open to the sky. A hundred years is nothing in the life of an oak. It will be 300 years in the growing and another 300 in the dying. But not these. These will be cut down, their space filled by heavy plant for the Council's heavier-handed bridge repair.

Go, go now! Pay your respects. Another month and they too will be gone.